The Magic Factory
TRICK OR TREAT?

Why not zoom out and buy Theresa Breslin's other
'Magic Factory' titles?

Cold Spell
Midsummer Magic

The Magic Factory

TRICK OR TREAT?

THERESA BRESLIN

OXFORD

UNIVERSITY PRESS

OXFORD

UNIVERSITY PRESS

Great Clarendon Street, Oxford OX2 6DP

Oxford University Press is a department of the University of Oxford.
It furthers the University's objective of excellence in research, scholarship,
and education by publishing worldwide in

Oxford New York

Auckland Cape Town Dar es Salaam Hong Kong Karachi
Kuala Lumpur Madrid Melbourne Mexico City Nairobi
New Delhi Shanghai Taipei Toronto

With offices in

Argentina Austria Brazil Chile Czech Republic France Greece
Guatemala Hungary Italy Japan Poland Portugal Singapore
South Korea Switzerland Thailand Turkey Ukraine Vietnam

Oxford is a registered trade mark of Oxford University Press
in the UK and in certain other countries

British Library Cataloguing in Publication Data
Data available

ISBN: 978-0-19-275450-9

1 3 5 7 9 10 8 6 4 2

Printed in Great Britain by
Cox & Wyman Ltd, Reading, Berkshire

This book is for Blair's class
St Bride's Primary
Bothwell

All manner of
Super Spells
and
Powerful
Potions

Bespoke Broomsticks
by the Bogle

SPECIAL DISCOUNT RATE FOR
EDUCATIONAL ESTABLISHMENTS

WE NUMBER AMONG OUR CLIENTS
THE ACADEMY OF ALCHEMISTS, AND
THE COLLEGE OF THE CRYSTAL BALL

NO ORDER TOO PECULIAR

Wand maintenance undertaken

Leaky cauldrons repaired

Crystal balls re-energized

Difficult and disobedient
dragons retrained

CONTENTS

Semolina Saves the Day

'BROOMSTICKS!'

The big gargoyle sitting on the windowsill of the Tallest Tower of Starling Castle shouted as loudly as he could.

'**Broomsticks!**' he shouted again. 'Heading this way!'

Midden, the little witch who was in charge of the Magic Factory inside the Tallest Tower of Starling Castle, rushed over to the window. 'Where are they, Growl?' she asked.

Growl the Gargoyle pointed to the high hills that surrounded Starling Castle. 'There,' he said. 'Can't you see?'

'I can see something far away above the mountain tops.' Midden screwed up her eyes. 'Dark shapes moving. Are you sure they're not just rain clouds?'

'Rain clouds?' growled Growl. 'I've been sitting on the window ledge of this castle for six hundred years. I know rain clouds when I see them. And I'm telling you, Midden, that's not rain clouds. That's broomsticks. Dozens of them, all coming here, to the Magic Factory shop, because it's the last shopping day before Hallowe'en.'

Midden pushed up her sleeves and groped through the pockets of her witch's cape.

From one pocket she took out a wad of everlasting green chewing gum, from another she pulled a crumpled Spell Scroll, in a third was her Wrong Riddle Book. Finally, in the last pocket, she found what she was looking for—her big round magic Seeing Spectacles.

Midden put on her Seeing Spectacles and jumped back.

Up close, Growl the Gargoyle was enormous and *very* scary.

Midden stuck her head out of the castle window and peered again at the high hills.

With her magic Seeing Spectacles Midden could see far away things as though they were right under her nose.

She saw the trees growing at the foot of the mountains as though they were at her feet.

She saw the snow shining white at the very top of the mountains as though it was on top of her own head.

And then she saw what Growl was pointing at.

'Sputtering spells!' she exclaimed.

A whole bevy of broomsticks were flying slap-bang towards her. Some were old-fashioned broomsticks chugging steadily through the sky, others were mega-magic-charged models thundering along. They were streaming in from all directions towards Starling Castle.

'You're right, Growl!' said Midden. 'Those *are* broomsticks.' The little witch pulled her head back inside the window. 'I'd better tell the rest of the team to get a move on. I'm in such a guddle, with loads of potions to put together and some spells to sort out.'

Suddenly there was a bubbling sound from the fireplace in the Magic Factory, and then a hissing noise.

'The cauldron's boiling over!' The Bogle, the big hairy beastie who was one of Midden's helpers in the Magic Factory and who had been mending a broomstick in the corner near the fire, stood up and waved his four arms about. 'Midden!' he cried again. 'The cauldron! It's boiling over!'

4

Midden ran back across the room. Bright orange liquid was frothing up over the edge of the cauldron and onto the fire. She grabbed the cauldron handle and swung it away from the flames.

'That's fast-acting luminous hair dye,' she said. 'I made it a vivid orange colour especially for Hallowe'en.'

'It will be a *burnt* orange colour then,' squawked Corbie the Clever Crow. He was another of Midden's team in the Magic Factory. 'Do you want a hand, or rather a wing, to bottle it up?'

'We've got *tons* of stuff to bottle and box and package and parcel and carry down the spiral staircase to the shop,' said Midden. 'The last few days have been so busy I can hardly keep up. Why does everyone always leave their Hallowe'en shopping to the very last minute? They know the Magic Factory works all year long preparing potions, discovering new spells, making magic clothes, mending cauldrons, and repairing broken broomsticks. And they know the Magic Factory Shop is always open. Yet they wait until the day before Hallowe'en, when we're rushed off our feet, before they decide to drop in.'

'Don't worry, Midden,' cawed Corbie. 'You've got me

and the Bogle and Cat and Semolina the Shape Shifter here to help you. We'll have most of it finished off and downstairs to the Magic Factory Shop before our customers arrive.'

'No problem,' said Semolina. 'Watch this!'

And Semolina the Shape Shifter, who was normally a puddingy kind of shape, changed herself into an octopus. She sat down at the big table in the Magic Factory and began to work, making up the recipes Midden had written out.

'*Broomstick Polish—Measure out seventeen Finkle Dots and add a drop of Dragon's Blood,*' Semolina read out, '*then stir with a Phoenix Feather.*'

She used two of her tentacles to do this, and a third to write a label and stick it to the bottle. At the same time two of her other tentacles were busy with the ingredients for the next recipe.

'*Smelly Jokes. Your friends won't see these coming! Take three spoonfuls*

of Invisible Oil . . . Where has that disappeared to?'
Semolina groped about on the table surface. 'Oh yes,
here it is. *Sprinkle in some Pongy Powder, shake well,
and wrap in Laughing Leaf.*'

Semolina's eight tentacles were a blur as she measured and cut and scooped and mixed and brewed and
cooked and poured.

'That's brilliant, Semolina,' said Corbie. 'As you finish each recipe I'll fly up and down the stairs with the goods.'

'And I'll go downstairs to the Magic Factory Shop, Midden,' said Cat, 'and arrange our merchandise in a tasteful display when Corbie brings it to me.'

Cat, whose full name was Cat-Astro-Phe, and who had been the royal cat of the Pharaohs in Ancient Egypt in one of her previous lives, liked to do tasks that didn't get her paws too dirty. She was a very elegant cat and Midden thought she would be the perfect person to set out the goods they had to sell.

'Thank you very much, Cat,' said Midden, 'and all the rest of you. I'll finish off bottling the instant orange hair dye.'

'Can I help too?' asked the Bogle, who was very good at fixing broomsticks but wasn't often allowed to handle magic potions.

'All right then,' said Midden. 'You hold the bottles in your hands and I'll ladle the hair dye into them from the cauldron.'

'Magical Fantastical!' said the Bogle.

Midden had just put the stopper on the last bottle of Hallowe'en Hair Dye when the first broomsticks soared overhead.

'That's Wizard Tangle Wangle coming in to land outside the shop now,' Growl the Gargoyle shouted from the windowsill, 'with the two old hags from the Highlands, Nanny Northwind and Goodwife MacGumboil.'

'I'll go down with the Bogle and help serve our customers,' Midden told Semolina.

The Bogle grabbed as many bottles of hair dye as he could carry with his four hands and raced out of the Magic Factory.

'I'll stay here,' said Semolina, 'and go on making up the recipes. Growl can keep me up to date with what's happening outside and the Bogle can come up and let me know which supplies are running out.'

Midden gathered up the potions and packets that Semolina had prepared and followed the Bogle down the spiral staircase of the Tallest Tower. She arrived in the Magic Factory Shop as the doorbell jangled and their first customers walked in.

'Happy Hallowe'en to you and your team, Midden!' cackled Nanny Northwind, taking her pipe out of her mouth and waving it at the little witch.

'Same to you,' said Midden, 'and to you, Goodwife MacGumboil,' she added as the other old hag from the Highlands hobbled into the shop.

'My legs are giving me gip,' moaned Goodwife MacGumboil. 'These long broomstick rides fair take it out of me. I'm not as young as I used to be.'

'Oh, stop complaining, you old hag.' Nanny Northwind gave her friend a hearty slap on the back. 'You know Midden's recipes and new spells are worth travelling all this way to buy.'

'Happy Hallowe'en to you, Wizard Tangle Wangle,' Corbie the Crow called out as an elderly wizard with a long white beard came into the shop.

'I've a new product this year,' Midden told her customers. 'Instant Orange Hair Dye fresh from my cauldron. Very seasonal colour.'

'I'm more interested in this,' said Nanny Northwind, lifting a packet labelled *Talking Vomit* from a shelf marked 'Hallowe'en Tricks'.

'Look what I've got!' shrieked Goodwife MacGumboil. 'It's fake dog poo that grows legs and runs away when you try to sweep it up!'

'Let's get a dozen each,' said Nanny Northwind, 'and cause a riot at the Highland Hallowe'en Ball tomorrow night.'

'Do you think I'd suit my beard dyed orange?' Wizard Tangle Wangle asked Cat.

'A wizard of your grandeur would look magnificent with an orange beard,' Cat told him, 'especially if you bought yourself a splendid new black cloak to set it off.'

'I've just the very thing for you, Wizard Tangle Wangle,' said Midden. 'It's full length with a peaked collar and a hem sewn with sparkling stars.'

The bell of the shop door pinged again and a pair of Spell Doctors and three small goblins came in, and then more and more witches and wizards and all kinds of magical folk.

The shop was crowded now, with everyone chatting together, exchanging news and making such a terrific noise that Midden didn't hear Growl the Gargoyle's next announcement, despite the fact that he made it in an especially loud voice.

'Boris and Cloris flying in,' bellowed Growl the Gargoyle. 'The twins from the college of the Crystal Ball.'

Growl didn't say, as he would have liked to, 'The *terrible* twins from the College of the Crystal Ball.'

Boris and Cloris were well known as the two most mischievous pupils that had ever attended the College.

As they flew past him on their beginners' broomsticks Growl put on one of his most severe looks. Being a gargoyle this meant that Growl's face was truly awful, but Boris and Cloris cheekily thumbed their noses at him.

The Magic Factory Shop was so full the twins couldn't push their way in and had to wait outside. As they parked their broomsticks Boris nudged Cloris.

'Look at *that* one with the mega-magic motor,' he said. 'It must be Wizard Tangle Wangle's broomstick.'

Cloris peered in the shop window. 'He's talking to Midden, the little witch. She's helping him try on a new wizard cloak.'

Boris glanced about him. At that moment they were

on their own outside the shop.

Cloris saw her twin looking around. 'Are you thinking what I'm thinking?' she asked him.

'I wouldn't mind a ride on that,' said Boris.

'Why don't we try it out?' Cloris suggested.

Boris nodded. 'We could go for a quick spin and have it back before he comes out and no one would be any the wiser.'

The twins climbed on to Wizard Tangle Wangle's broomstick.

'It's not got a safety harness,' Boris said as they settled themselves down.

'Phooey!' scoffed Cloris. 'Who needs a safety harness? Are you scared?'

'Never!' said Boris and pressed the start button.

Cat was reaching out a dainty paw to pick up a bottle of Midden's new Instant Orange Hallowe'en Hair Dye to wrap for Wizard Tangle Wangle when there was an almighty bang from outside the shop door.

'Eeeek!' screeched Cat and the bottle of hair dye

catapulted into the air. The stopper came loose and the orange dye splattered all over Cat. 'My fur!' Cat yowled in horror. 'My beautiful fur!'

'What was *that*?' Midden looked out of the shop window just in time to see Wizard Tangle Wangle's broomstick roaring into the air.

'My broomstick!' cried Wizard Tangle Wangle, running towards the door but tripping on his new cloak and dragging Midden, who was still holding it, with him.

Cat, with orange hair dye in her eyes, leapt off the counter on top of the Bogle, who threw his four arms in the air, swiping out at Corbie, who flapped his wings, catching Nanny Northwind round the ear, and she fell over, clattering Goodwife MacGumboil and several small goblins to the floor.

Outside the shop Wizard Tangle Wangle's broomstick streaked skywards with the twins clinging on to the handle.

'Help!!!!!!' shrieked Boris and Cloris.

From his position on the windowsill of the Tallest Tower of Starling Castle, Growl the Gargoyle caught sight of the twins' terrified faces as they rocketed past him at a hundred magic miles an hour.

'Get over here pronto!' Growl yelled through the window of the Tallest Tower to Semolina the Shape Shifter who was still working away furiously.

Semolina realized she couldn't run very fast as an octopus, so she shape-shifted herself into her usual puddingy person with arms and legs and ran across the room.

'What's the matter?' she said.

'That's what's the matter!' Growl pointed his claw.

High above Starling Castle Wizard Tangle Wangle's broomstick was looping the loop at supersonic speed.

'It's the terrible twins,' said Growl. 'They're on that runaway broomstick. If we don't do something they're going to be killed!'

Downstairs in the shop Midden and the other magical folk were a mass of arms and legs and paws and claws all jammed in the shop doorway with an orange Cat as they tried to get out.

Midden managed to pull herself free. 'Come with me!' she called to her team of helpers. Closely followed by Cat, Corbie, and the Bogle, the little witch ran through to the back of the shop and up the spiral staircase to the Magic Factory.

Boris and Cloris had never been on a mega-magicked powered broomstick before, not even as passengers. They had only ever ridden low-power broomsticks and even then were supposed to wear safety harnesses if using anything above a Level Three. They could hardly keep themselves seated on board Wizard Tangle Wangle's broomstick, never mind try to steer or control it.

'There must be a cruise control button.' Cloris's teeth were rattling in her head as she tried to hold on and look at the broomstick control panel.

'Can you see an automatic pilot lever or anything?' Boris's whole body juddered.

The broomstick swung in another enormous arc.

'I can't hang on much longer,' Cloris said to her twin in a shaky scared voice.

'Me neither,' whimpered Boris.

They both looked down. They were high in the air directly above the hard cobblestones of the main courtyard of Starling Castle.

Then Wizard Tangle Wangle's broomstick shuddered violently.

Boris and Cloris screamed as they lost their grip and began to fall to the ground.

Midden and her team rushed into the Magic Factory and over to the window.

'Oh no!' gasped Midden as she saw the twins falling.

In the next instant Semolina the Shape Shifter

jumped from the windowsill of the Tallest Tower.

As she flung herself towards the castle courtyard Semolina changed her shape. From her puddingy person shape she became a rocket which went faster than the twins were falling. She raced past them, and just as she reached earth, Semolina changed to become round and flat.

'What's she doing?' cried Midden.

The next moment they could all see exactly what Semolina had become.

A huge trampoline.

Just in time. Three seconds later Boris and Cloris reached the ground. Or rather they didn't reach the ground. They landed on the trampoline, and . . .

They bounced . . .

And bounced again.

When Boris and Cloris had bounced up and down a few times they tried to stop bouncing so that they could climb off.

But Semolina had other plans for them. She curled her trampoline shape up at each side and made herself extra springy. Semolina knew that the twins were so naughty that if she let them go they would soon be up to more mischief. She decided to keep Boris and Cloris bouncing up and down until Midden had flown up on her own broomstick and thrown a tow rope round Wizard Tangle Wangle's broomstick and hauled it back down to the Magic Factory so that the Bogle could check it out. After she had done that Midden had to make another batch of luminous orange dye for Wizard Tangle Wangle to use on his beard, and a special spell to remove orange stains from Cat's fur.

The twins were made to apologize to everybody and then they were given back their own broomsticks. But the Bogle had made some adjustments so that they could only fly at a very low level and slow speed.

And when Boris and Cloris were finally allowed into the Magic Factory Shop to look at the Hallowe'en goodies, they found that all that was left for them to buy was a handbook with the title *Beginners Guide to Flying Broomsticks.*

The Dancing Skeletons

'This is going to be the best Hallowe'en Party ever,' said Midden.

The little witch was hovering on her broomstick above the chandelier in the Great Hall of Starling Castle. Below her, the big hairy beastie known as the Bogle was holding a bundle of spooky decorations ready to be hung up.

In one hand he had a long row of white skeleton cut outs. In another hand he had a packet of drawing pins. In his third and fourth hands he held lengths of grey musty cobweb.

'Have you got a pair of scissors there?' Midden asked him. She was fastening an enormous hollowed-out pumpkin to the chandelier with a piece of string.

The Bogle checked each of his four hands. 'Nope,' he said.

'Drat!' said Midden. 'I need to cut off this string. I don't want it hanging down onto the floor in case any of the children pull on it. We have to make sure that it's safely out of their reach when the candles are lit inside the pumpkin.'

'I could make a pair of scissors appear,' the Bogle said eagerly. He put the thumb and middle finger of his third hand together and tried to click them the way Midden sometimes did when she was making magic.

'Er . . . no, Bogle,' Midden said quickly. The Bogle was still learning how to do magic and often made mistakes. 'It would be better if you brought me the ones from the Magic Factory.'

Midden whizzed back a bit on her broomstick to make sure the pumpkin was in the right place. 'Let's see how it will look tonight,' she said.

Midden snapped her fingers.

There was a fizzle.

Like this—*fIZZZZZZZZZZ!!!!!!!*

Then . . . a loud pop!

Like that—*pop!*

Suddenly an orange flame appeared on top of each candle inside the pumpkin. The Great Hall lit up with a warm glow.

'Isn't that lovely?' Midden said to the Bogle.

The Bogle looked round the Great Hall. He smiled and nodded his hairy head. He loved parties, especially Hallowe'en parties. He thought about the fun and games they were going to have. And when he looked up at the chandelier he felt that the warm glow he could see there was inside him as well as inside the pumpkin lantern.

'When it's dark tonight the Great Hall will look Magical Fantastical.' The Bogle's face beamed in a happy smile.

'Yes,' said Midden. 'But I really do need to cut the string. Be a good Bogle and run off and fetch the scissors, would you, please?'

The Bogle groaned and mumbled, but he put the

decorations down on the floor and lumbered off to find the scissors.

Midden pressed a button on her broomstick so that it would circle in the air, and she made up a little song as she waited for the Bogle to return.

'I do like Hallowe'en,
What a lovely scene!
Going out at night,
All by candlelight!

Dressing up is fun,
Scaring everyone;
Lovely things to eat,
As we play "Trick or Treat?"!'

Midden rummaged in the pockets of her witch's cape until she found her 'to do' list. She counted off her jobs for the day.

1. Fasten hollowed-out pumpkin to chandelier.
2. Pin rows of white card skeletons round the walls.

 3. Hang lengths of musty cobweb everywhere.

The little witch put a big tick beside the first item on her list.

The Bogle didn't like running errands.

It really was *awfully* far for him to walk back to the Magic Factory workshops in Starling Castle to fetch the scissors. He was tired from the work he'd already done today. Why didn't Midden use magic to bring the scissors to her? And why not make more magic to hang up the Hallowe'en decorations.

The Bogle had asked Midden that question this afternoon when they were carrying the Hallowe'en decorations across the castle courtyard to the Great Hall.

'The rules for magic are decided at the Magicians' Management Meetings,' Midden explained, 'and the last rule book they sent out said that magic shouldn't be wasted on silly things. So it's best to keep our magic for making potions and spells in the Magic Factory and not use it as an excuse to be lazy. Besides which, Bogle, if we used magic to do everything that needed doing

I think that you might never get out of bed.'

To the Bogle, never getting out of bed seemed a great idea. He liked lying in bed in the morning . . .

. . . and in the afternoon,

. . . and in the evening,

. . . and at night time.

But now, instead of doing that, he had to walk across the courtyard, past the well and down to the Deepest Dungeon of the castle. Then he would have to go through the Hidden Door, along the Secret Passage, through the shop, and up and up the spiral staircase until he reached the top of the Tallest Tower.

Inside the Tallest Tower was the Magic Factory—and the scissors that Midden wanted the Bogle to fetch. They would be lying on the worktable where he had left them this morning.

The Bogle came out of the Great Hall into the courtyard. From here he could see that the window of the top room in the Tallest Tower was lying open. And what's more, Growl the Gargoyle was not in his usual place on the windowsill. Every member of the

Magic Factory team was doing some task or other to prepare for the Starling Castle Hallowe'en Party tonight.

The Bogle breathed in deeply. It was a wonderfully sparkly kind of a day . . . the kind of day that was absolutely right for magic. Perhaps he could make a tiny spell to save him such a long walk. It would only be a *tiny* spell. He'd still be doing what Midden asked him, so that would be all right, wouldn't it?

The Bogle looked about the courtyard. It was very quiet. No witches or wizards flying by on their broomsticks, no one gathering magical herbs in the castle gardens, nobody trying out a new spell anywhere. No one around to see him. Midden would never find out. Today of all days there was so much magic about she'd never notice a little extra. Would she?

Back in the Great Hall there was a swirl of air and the door opened. Count Countalot who ran the Castle Café came in carrying several trays of food.

'Hello, Midden.' He waved to the little witch as he set the trays down on the tables at one end of the room. Midden tucked her 'to do' list into a pocket of her witch's cape and swooped down on her broomstick to have a look.

The trays from the Castle Café were piled high with delicious food. There were slime sandwiches, witch and wizard hat biscuits, and bogey bagels with worm spaghetti dip. There were plates of pickled eggs that looked like eyeballs, and pieces of white cheese smeared with dark mustard to look like rotten teeth. There were stinky sausage rolls and lots and lots of sweets in the shapes of bats and spiders. Right in the middle of the table Count Countalot placed a large Hallowe'en cake made to look like Starling Castle and decorated with black and silver icing.

'The sandwiches look absolutely horrible,' said Midden in admiration.

'They *are* gorgeously gruesome,' agreed Count Countalot. 'The staff in the café have been mixing and baking since early morning. We've still got the treacle scones and the basins of apples to bring in but we're about to have a tea break now. Fancy a cuppa?'

'That's a good idea,' said Midden. 'I think I will. The Bogle has gone to fetch a pair of scissors and you know how long it takes the Bogle to do something he doesn't want to.'

So Midden went off to the Castle Café for tea.

'I'll make sure the door is closed properly,' said the Count as they left the Great Hall together. On his way out he slammed the door shut behind him.

Inside the Great Hall the chandelier shuddered. The enormous pumpkin swayed from side to side. Inside the pumpkin one of the candles fell over. The flame flared up and made more flames.

Soon fire would be climbing up the chandelier towards the roof of the Great Hall.

The Bogle wasn't very good at magic. He forgot spells almost as soon as he heard them. The words always got mixed up in his head. But he only wanted a pair of scissors to come to him. Surely it was perfectly simple to get a pair of scissors to do what he wanted?

The Bogle stood in the middle of the castle court-yard, pointed at the open window of the top room in the Tallest Tower and chanted:

> '*Scissors, walking you will be,*
> *Scissors, scissors, come to me.*'

The Bogle waited.

Nothing happened.

Was there another word he should have said? Of course! There was a very famous magic word. How did it go again?

'Abra,' began the Bogle. 'Erm . . . Abra . . . cad . . .' He paused. 'Abra . . . cad . . . ab . . . adeebee . . . dozy,' he said.

There was no sign of any movement from the open window.

If he wanted the scissors to come to him he would need something else. The Bogle put one of his hands down the inside of his left purple boot. This was where he kept his little bag of Magic Dust for emergencies. Using his first and second hands he opened up the bag and took out some Magic Dust. That should do the trick.

The Bogle put a small amount of the Magic Dust

on the palm of his third hand and covered it with his fourth so that it wouldn't blow away. He held these hands very still while he used his first two hands to tie up the bag and put it back in his left boot. When he had tucked the bag safely out of sight he opened up hands three and four. The grains of dust shone and glittered.

The Bogle took a deep breath. Then he blew the Magic Dust as far as he could in the direction of the open window of the Tallest Tower and repeated his poem:

'Scissors, walking you will be,
Scissors, scissors, come to me!'

The Bogle waited.

His ears began to tingle. There was definitely magic in the air!

Then the window of the Tallest Tower crashed wide open. Two big eyes peered out. They were the open circles of the handles of the scissors!

'Oh, Magical Fantastical!' said the Bogle in excitement. 'It's working! My spell is working!'

The next moment the scissors stepped out of the

window and stood up on the points of their blades on the window ledge.

The Bogle looked round again to make sure no one had come into the courtyard. He waved his four arms in the air. 'Come on, scissors,' he called out. 'Down here! Come down here!'

Snip, snip.

The blades of the scissors opened and closed. They jumped out of the window and turned sideways onto their points.

Snip, snip, the scissors walked briskly down the wall of the Tallest Tower.

Snip, snip, snip.

When they reached the ground the scissors gave a little skip and a hop and stood up straight on the cobblestones.

The Bogle beckoned to them. 'Now come over here to me,' he said.

'Brilliant,' said the Bogle as the scissors marched towards him. He pointed to the Great Hall. 'We're going in there,' he said. 'You're needed to cut some string.'

When the scissors reached him the Bogle stretched out two of his hands to grasp the handles.

But the scissors did not stop.

Snip, snip.

The scissors clicked past him.

'Bother,' said the Bogle, and he reached out his other two hands to grab the scissors.

Snip, snip.

The scissors strode away, getting faster and faster.

Now a Bogle has four arms. And if you have four arms then you have four hands, and that can be very useful. It means that you can pick your nose, scratch your head, and eat your dinner—all at the same time. But today the Bogle would have liked a few more pairs of hands.

Even though he used hands one, two, three, and four, he could not catch the speeding scissors. He could only run after them as they *snip, snip, snipped* their way into the Great Hall.

The Bogle was so relieved that Midden wasn't in the Great Hall to see the scissors running on their own he didn't notice anything else.

The flames from the pumpkin had reached up through the chandelier and were licking along the wooden beams. The ceiling was about to catch fire!

But the Bogle didn't hear the noise nor notice the smell because he was too busy chasing the scissors. He tried to think of a way to make the scissors stop. He chanted another rhyme.

'Scissors, scissors, rest at ease.
Scissors, no more walking please!'

'*Please!*' he cried out loud.

But the scissors ignored him and kept marching round the Great Hall.

Snip, snip.

The scissors came to where the spooky decorations lay in a pile on the floor.

Snip, snip.

They stopped and peered at the white cardboard skeletons.

'Oh no!' shouted the Bogle. He remembered

he had told the scissors that they were needed to cut some string.

Snip, snip,snip!

The scissors cut the string tying the white cardboard skeletons together.

Snip! snip!

They marched away.

Then, to the Bogle's astonishment, one by one and very unsteadily, the skeletons got to their feet. They straightened up their bony bodies and began to stagger after the scissors!

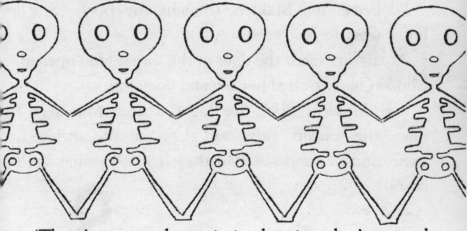

'There's too much magic in the air today,' moaned the Bogle.

He tried to trip up the nearest skeleton but it only

laughed a hollow laugh. Then it pointed a skinny finger at him and, with a rattle of bones, it waltzed away to join its friends.

Soon all the bony beings were following the scissors in a crazy conga line round and round the Great Hall.

'Stop! Stop!' shrieked the Bogle.

But the neither the skeletons nor the scissors paid any attention.

I'd better tell Midden, thought the Bogle. She'll know what to do.

At that moment the door of the Great Hall opened. Midden had finished her tea and come back.

'Oh, Midden!' cried the Bogle. 'I need your help. I made the scissors walk, and they cut the skeletons loose, and . . . and . . . now they won't do what I tell them!'

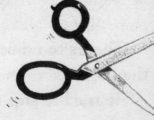

Midden saw dozens of skeletons dancing round the room following a pair of scissors.

Then Midden sniffed the air. She could smell smoke. She looked up. She saw the flames coming from the pumpkin going up towards the ceiling.

'Oh, I see what you've been trying to do!' she cried.

'You do?' said the Bogle.

'Yes, of course,' said Midden. 'What a clever idea to use the skeletons to put out the fire. Let me help you.' She took her magic wand from behind her ear and waved it at the skeletons.

Zippity Zap!!!

At once the skeletons turned and danced out of the Great Hall into the courtyard. They ran over to the well. One of them lowered the bucket and filled it with water.

Count Countalot looked out of the window of the Castle Café and saw what was happening. He rushed out with more buckets and basins.

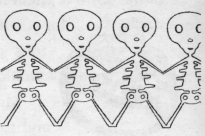

The skeletons formed a line from the well to the Great Hall and began to pass the buckets and basins along. Even the scissors tried to help.

The Bogle stood inside the Great Hall and, using his four arms, he passed the buckets and basins full of water up to Midden. Midden flew backwards and forwards on her broomstick throwing water onto the flames.

Very soon the fire was under control. When the last of the flames had been put out the skeletons and the scissors collapsed in a heap.

After everything had been cleared up the Bogle spoke to Midden. 'I think I should tell you,' he said. 'I was trying out a spell, and it went wrong, and—'

Midden held her hand up. 'Don't say any more,' she told the Bogle. 'It was my fault. I went away and left the candles lit inside the pumpkin. It was very careless of me. One of them must have fallen over. If it wasn't for you making the scissors and the skeletons come alive the whole building would have caught fire.'

Midden pointed to the pumpkin and to the ceiling. Some of the beams were a bit scorched but the fire was out and the chandelier and the castle were safe.

'But . . .' said the Bogle.

'Never mind any buts,' said Midden.

'I . . . I . . . should explain,' said the Bogle.

'No,' said Midden. 'You don't need to explain anything. You saved the Great Hall from burning down. I will make a special announcement tonight. You'll get a big round of applause, Bogle. Everyone will know that it's thanks to you that we can have our Hallowe'en Party this year.'

'You are a very clever Bogle,' Midden added.

'I am?' said the Bogle.

Then he nodded his hairy head in agreement.

'I *am*,' he said.

Trick or Treat?

'You'll be extra careful with these magic tricks, Growl, won't you?'

Midden, the little witch who was in charge of the Magic Factory at Starling Castle, handed Growl the Gargoyle a large box.

'It has to go to Professor Pernickety at the Multi-Story School,' she explained. 'He ordered a box of mixed tricks so that his pupils can have a lucky Hallowe'en dip today.'

Growl took the box from Midden and gripped it tightly in his claws. 'What kind of magic tricks did you make for them this year?'

'I put in some of the old favourites,' said Midden, 'the ones the children like so much.'

'Never-ending chocolate bars?' growled Growl, licking his lips.

'Lots of those.' Midden nodded. 'And coins that vanish and reappear behind your ear, and paper hankies that sneeze by themselves. But I've added some new magic tricks for the children to try out. There's a list of contents on the lid.'

'*Exploding Eyeballs and Slime-Squirting Sweets!*' Growl read from the top of the box. 'Brilliant! Let's have a look.' He began to open the lid with one of his claws.

'Oh no, Growl!' said Midden. 'Please don't open it right now. We've been so busy this Hallowe'en that I've only just finished making these tricks. The magic hasn't completely bound together yet. That's why you'll need to be especially gentle when carrying it. Let Professor Pernickety know that the box must not be opened for at least another hour. By that time the tricks will be ready to work properly.'

The Magic Factory, where Midden and her team of

helpers mixed their magic and stirred up spells, was in the Tallest Tower of Starling Castle.

Growl's job was to sit on the windowsill and act as lookout. When he wanted to go into Starling village Growl climbed up to the flagpole on the Tallest Tower. He'd swing round and round before letting go to fly through the air onto the roof of the Great Hall. From there he'd slide down a handy drainpipe, scuttle across the courtyard, and ask Jamie the Drawbridge Keeper to lower the drawbridge.

As soon as Jamie turned the handle and the drawbridge creaked open, Growl would tramp across to the Multi-Story School just outside the Castle Gate.

Growl really liked jumping about on the rooftops and swinging from the flagpole, but he decided that might not be a good idea while carrying the box of magic tricks. So today he left the Magic Factory by going down the spiral staircase inside the Tallest Tower and out through the shop. Then he went along the Secret Passage, and opened the Hidden Door into the Deepest Dungeon. From there he climbed the stairs to the main part of the castle and walked slowly across the courtyard to the castle entrance.

'Hi, Growl. Happy Hallowe'en,' said Jamie. 'What have you got there?'

'A box of magic tricks.' Growl tapped the lid with his claw. 'Midden says there are enough tricks for every pupil in the Multi-Story School to play "Trick or Treat?" tonight.'

Jamie looked at the list of contents. '*Burping Biscuits?*' he said. 'Never heard of them. What do they do?'

'Dunno,' said Growl. 'Must be one of the new magic tricks that Midden said she'd made for Hallowe'en this year.'

Jamie bent closer to see. 'Bite on a Burping Biscuit!' he read out. 'Munch it in your mouth. Stand back. A burp will erupt. Then the biscuit will say, "Pardon *me!*"'

'Oh, the kids will love those,' said Growl.

'Can I have a quick peek?' asked Jamie.

Growl shook his head. 'Midden told me the box mustn't be opened for another hour. She said the ingredients and the spells are still blending, and the magic needs more time to set.'

As Growl and Jamie were speaking, the lid of the box began to jiggle up and down.

'It's almost as though they know we're talking about them,' whispered Jamie. He lowered the drawbridge and let Growl pass through.

Giggles, more giggles, and then a very loud sneeze sounded from inside the box. Growl pressed the lid down firmly. He kept one stone hand on the top of the box while he trundled over the drawbridge towards the Multi-Story School.

'One box of Mixed Tricks. Sign here, please.'

As Professor Pernickety of the Multi-Story Nursery School signed the delivery note the school children rushed over to see what Growl had brought. They knew they would each be given a trick and wanted to have them right away. There were huge sighs of disappointment when Growl explained that they would have to wait at least an hour before the box could be opened.

Growl was upset to see the children so disappointed. He made a quick funny face and they began to laugh. Then he made another and they laughed even more.

'I've an idea,' said Professor Pernickety. 'If Growl is not in a hurry to get back to the Magic Factory perhaps he'd like to stay for a bit and make some more funny faces for us.'

'Please, Growl,' the children begged. 'Say yes. *Please.*'

'It would keep the children amused until it's time to open the box,' Professor Pernickety added.

'Oh well . . . ' said Growl.

Growl was great at being a gargoyle and he loved his job. But working with the team at the Magic Factory and being a lookout at the top of the Tallest Tower meant that he didn't get to meet many people. The ones he did meet were mainly witches and wizards and the occasional genie. But Growl liked to talk to ordinary people every once in a while, and he especially liked making odd faces and hearing children laugh.

'Oh, well. All right, then,' said Growl. 'Yes, I'll make some funny faces until it's time to open the box of tricks.'

Professor Pernickety ushered the children into the school assembly hall. The little ones, the Infants, sat at the front of the hall. The middle-sized children, the

Juniors, sat in the middle. And the older children, the Seniors, sat at the back. They shuffled their chairs to get a good position to see Growl making his best gargoyle faces.

Professor Pernickety put the box of magic tricks behind the screen at the back of the hall and then he sat down at the front with the little children to watch Growl.

Growl let his arms fall to his sides so that his claws scraped along the floor as he ambled on to the stage. Then he lifted one arm and waved to his audience.

'Make a really horrible face for us, please, Growl,' one of the junior children called out.

'It might be too scary for the little ones,' said Growl.

'Please! Please!' the Seniors and the Juniors and the Infant classes shouted together.

Growl looked at Professor Pernickety.

'Oh, why not?' Professor Pernickety nodded his head. 'It *is* Hallowe'en, after all.'

Growl stood at the front of the stage. First of all he stuck out his tongue.

All the children clapped politely, but Growl could

see that some of the older ones had expected a more frightening face.

Growl stuck his tongue out some more. Out and out and out and out, came Growl's tongue.

The children gasped.

Longer and thinner and thinner and longer, Growl's tongue curled up round behind his neck and back to the front of his face. Then he flicked it up so that it snaked inside his left nostril!

'Disgusting!' the children screamed. 'Do it again!'

So Growl did. But this time his tongue went inside his *right* nostril.

'Now tell me if you like this one,' said Growl. He popped his eyeballs almost right out of their sockets.

'Yuck!' said Professor Pernickety.

'Yes!' said the children.

Next Growl made his hair stand on end and waggled his eyebrows up and down.

'Fantastic!' yelled the children.

Growl puffed up his cheeks and flapped both his ears forwards.

This time the applause was louder.

'Can you pull your bottom lip up over your nose?' one of the Seniors asked Growl.

'I'll have a go,' said Growl.

This is a very difficult face to do and not every gargoyle is able to do it.

'Let's make this the last one,' said Professor Pernickety. 'It's almost time to open up the box of magic tricks.'

The children watched fascinated as Growl began to make his bottom lip wider and wider.

All the children, that is, except two.

Bad George and Rude Arabella.

Bad George and Rude Arabella were the two most badly behaved children in the Multi-Story School.

Not a day went by without Bad George getting into some sort of mischief. In fact, not even *half* a day went by without Bad George being in trouble.

As for Rude Arabella, no one was sure if she'd ever said a polite word in all the time she had been at the Multi-Story School.

Bad George and Rude Arabella had noticed

Professor Pernickety put the box of magic tricks behind the screen at the back of the assembly hall.

As soon as he saw that Professor Pernickety's attention was taken up with Growl making strange faces, George began to sidle over to the screen.

While the other children were laughing at Growl sticking his tongue up his nose, Rude Arabella edged towards the screen where the box of tricks had been placed.

When Professor Pernickety burst out laughing at Growl's expressions Bad George slipped behind the

screen. One second later Rude Arabella was also behind the screen.

'Go away, you,' Rude Arabella said rudely. 'I want to look at the box of tricks all by myself.'

'I was here first,' said Bad George. 'I want to see what kind of tricks are inside the box.'

He grabbed the box and began to read from the label on the lid. 'List of contents,' he said. 'Burping Biscuits; Bats that tell Batty Jokes; Spiders that spin Candy Floss; Exploding Eyeballs; Slime Squirting Sweets; Talking Sick. Ugh!'

He screwed up his face. 'What's Talking Sick?' he asked Rude Arabella.

'Oh, *everyone* knows what that is,' said Arabella. 'It's plastic sick and when you throw it on the ground it shouts "Barf! Barf!"' She pulled the box towards her so that she could see the label. 'Is that all there is?' She covered her mouth with her hand and made a rude yawning sound. 'Fake poo that runs away when you come near it? The same old boring tricks as last year. Yawn. Yawn.'

'There's other stuff too,' said Bad George. 'Hair ribbons and shoelaces that tie themselves into knots which can't be undone.' He pulled the box back towards him. 'And footballs that score a goal no matter where you kick them. I want one of *those*.'

'Well, hard cheese,' Rude Arabella told Bad George. 'You know Professor Pernickety doesn't allow choosing. Everybody puts their hand in without looking and you're stuck with whatever you get.' She yanked the box out of George's hand.

Suddenly there was a noise from inside the box. A scraping jostling sound—as if something was trying to escape.

'What was that?' asked Bad George.

'How should I know?' said Rude Arabella.

Bad George peered over her shoulder. 'There's something else written on the lid,' he told her. 'In big letters.'

MAGIC GOODS –
to be handled with care
To be opened under adult supervision

'That's rubbish,' said Rude Arabella rudely. 'It doesn't matter.'

'Only trying to spoil our fun,' agreed Bad George.

'It's not going to stop *me* looking,' said Rude Arabella.

Bad George and Rude Arabella took the lid off the box of magic tricks.

Inside the box the contents were simmering and bubbling.

'Seems harmless to me,' said Bad George.

An eye rolled up to the surface to look at them. It was a red eyeball in a pool of green liquid.

Rude Arabella reached out her hand to take it.

'I saw it first,' said Bad George.

'Don't care if you did,' said Rude Arabella. 'I'm having it.'

She grabbed the eyeball.

George tried to grab it at the same time. He gave Arabella a shove.

She gave him a push.

They both stuck out their elbows.

CRASH!

The box tipped over.

On the stage of the assembly hall, Growl the Gargoyle was just about to pull his bottom lip up over his nose when there was a CRASH! from behind the screen.

'Yipes!' Bad George yelped.

Professor Pernickety leaped to his feet.

With loud cries of 'Trick or Treat? Trick or Treat?' a great boiling mass of magic spells erupted through the school assembly hall.

'Look what you've done!'
cried Rude Arabella.

'It wasn't me!' said George.

'Was too!' said Arabella.

'Was not!' said George.

'Was! Was! Was!' Arabella screeched.

The other children jumped up from their seats as mixed-up magic tricks scattered in all directions.

The frogs were flying and the bats were hopping.

The spiders were burping while the biscuits exploded.

Eyeballs pinged off lamp shades.

Slimy sweets splatted against the windows.

The bars of chocolate sneezed as they rolled along the floor.

One of the frogs turned into a prince. He ran about shouting, 'Barf, barf! Barf, barf!'

Growl snapped his face back into his normal ugly expression.

'I'd better fetch Midden,' he said.

People think that gargoyles can't move very quickly

because they're made of stone but that's not true. Growl galloped up to the drawbridge and into the castle at top speed.

'Emergency!' he bawled to Jamie the Drawbridge Keeper. 'Midden needs to fly over to the Multi-Story School at once. The box of tricks has exploded!'

While Growl headed back to the Multi-Story School to try to help, Jamie ran into the courtyard and shouted up to the Tallest Tower.

'Midden! You're needed at the Multi-Story School!'

Midden jammed on her hat, jumped on her broom-stick, and jetted out of the Tower window in the direction of the school.

The assembly hall of the Multi-Story School was in absolute chaos.

Children were hiding under their chairs as blobs of pretend poo and fake sick chased each other round the room. Professor Pernickety and Growl were trying to calm the little ones when Midden zoomed in on her broomstick.

Growl clutched at an eyeball as it streaked past.

'Wheee!' said the eyeball dodging out of his reach. 'This is fun!'

Midden pulled her magic wand from behind her ear. '*Flippety Flop!*' she cried out. '*Make it stop!*'

Midden waved her magic wand.

Zippety Zap!!!

At once all the tricks stopped moving. Except for the shoelaces which wound themselves round Bad George's ankles, and the hair ribbons, which tied up Rude Arabella's legs so that she couldn't run away.

Midden looked at the terrible mess.

Flumps of sick were hanging from the ceiling, two paper hankies were stuffed in Growl's ears, and a large piece of fake poo sat on top of Professor Pernickety's head.

Midden muttered under her breath.

'Which spell to fix these mixed-up tricks?
I'll need more than one before I'm done.'

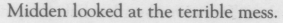

It took Midden *six* spells before she could untangle the mixed-up tricks. And even then she couldn't get the handsome prince to change back into a frog until she'd promised him that he could come to the Hallowe'en party that night at Starling Castle.

Then it took Midden *ten* different spells to make up some more tricks for the children to enjoy for their Hallowe'en treat.

Bad George and Rude Arabella had to stay behind after school. First they had to apologize to Midden and

Growl. Then Professor Pernickety made them sweep up the mess in the assembly hall. It took them *ages* to scrub the sticky slime from the windows and remove the grungey goo from the floor.

As for the squelchy stuff on the chair seats—don't even ask!

The Hallowe'en Party

'Just a teensy-weensy bit more Magic Dust, Midden, *please.*'

The Bogle held out his bag hopefully.

'Don't you have any left?' asked Midden, peering into the Bogle's bag.

'Only a tiny amount,' said the Bogle, 'and I do want to have fun at the Hallowe'en Party tonight.'

Midden opened the drawer of her desk and took out a golden key. She went to the big cupboard that stood on one side of the fireplace in the Magic Factory. Very special magical things were kept in this cupboard. Things like a pair of Seven League Boots, an Invisibility Cloak, and a jar of Magic Dust.

Midden unlocked the cupboard with her golden key and took down the jar of Magic Dust. 'I'll give you some more Magic Dust,' she said to the Bogle. 'It *is* Hallowe'en after all.'

'Goodeee!' said the Bogle as Midden measured out some of the sparkly powder into his Boglebag.

Midden put the stopper firmly back on the jar and replaced it on the shelf. The Bogle tied up his bag of Magic Dust and stuffed it down the side of his left Bogle boot.

'I'm going to have *lots* of fun at tonight's Hallowe'en Party,' he said.

'We all will,' said Midden. 'There's plenty of magic about to make sure that *everyone* has fun. Come on, let's get dressed up, the others are waiting. I can hear Jamie the Drawbridge Keeper tuning up his bagpipes. Our guests will be here soon and we should all be there in the castle courtyard to meet them and wish them a Happy Hallowe'en.'

Midden had already changed into her very best

witch's dress. It was full length with a long train and three hundred glittering black sequins. Midden took off her everyday witch's hat and put on her extra pointy super-duper one.

Lots of ordinary people dressed up as witches to celebrate Hallowe'en. So if you were a *real* witch, as Midden was, then you had to make a special effort.

Midden's hat for grand occasions was midnight black with silver spider's webs draped all over it.

The Bogle loved bright colours. For tonight's party he was wearing his red trousers, purple Bogle boots, and a yellow tartan waistcoat.

'You look amazing, Bogle,' said Midden as she helped him button up his waistcoat.

'You too, Midden,' the Bogle told her.

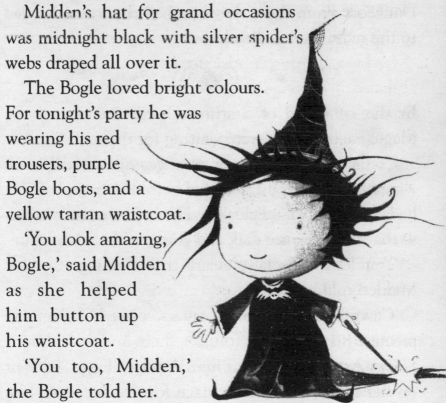

Midden tucked her magic wand behind her ear, pulled her witch's cape over her shoulders, grabbed one of the Bogle's four hands, and they were ready to leave.

They left the Magic Factory in the Tallest Tower of Starling Castle by going down the spiral staircase and out through the shop. Then they went along the Secret Passage and opened the Hidden Door into the Deepest Dungeon. From there they climbed the stairs that led to the main part of the castle.

In the courtyard of Starling Castle the rest of the Magic Factory team were waiting for them.

Corbie the Clever Crow was wearing a small black wizard hat with bright stars that twinkled on and off. He had on a short wizard cloak and he had oiled his feathers so that they gleamed dark and glossy in the moonlight.

'You look especially smart this evening, Corbie,' Midden told him.

'Cawfully kind of you to say so,' cawed Corbie, and preened his feathers.

Cat-Astro-Phe, the cat from Ancient Egypt, had put on her best Pharaoh's necklace for the occasion. She looked like a cat princess with her chain of gold and precious jewels draped around her neck.

'And you look really regal,' Midden said to Cat.

'Why, thank meow-you,' Cat purred with pleasure.

Semolina the Shape Shifter, who was normally a kind of pudding shape with legs, had changed herself into a beautiful fairy with silver wings.

'Semolina,' said Midden, 'that's a wonderful shape change! No one could tell that you're not a real fairy.'

Semolina laughed, and it sounded like the tinkle of fairy bells.

Growl the Gargoyle had twisted up his face to look absolutely awful. His nose was turned all the way up to his eyebrows and his mouth was turned all the way down to his chin.

'And you are the ugliest I've seen you for ages, Growl,' said Midden.

'Ta,' Growl growled.

Along the ramparts of Starling Castle rows of torches burned brightly. Coloured lights in the shape of moons and stars were strung between the towers and turrets.

Every window was lit up and the drawbridge had been lowered so that the party guests would be able to cross the moat to come inside the castle.

Every year on the night of the thirty-first of October the Magic Factory held a Hallowe'en Party in the Great Hall of Starling Castle. Midden had written out the invitations, and, last week, Corbie had delivered them. Everyone who lived nearby was invited to dress up and come along.

Suddenly there was a loud squealing noise.

Jamie the Drawbridge Keeper had begun to play a tune on his bagpipes. The first guests were arriving!

First came Professor Pernickety form the Multi-Story School. He was dressed up as Doctor Dolittle. His tall hat teetered on his head as he walked across the drawbridge.

Then his pupils and their families arrived. They were in dozens of different guises: aliens with two heads; clowns with cheery and sad faces; mummies wrapped in bandages; scarecrows and superheroes; monsters and knights; characters from storybooks;

heroes from films and television; and of course lots of witches and wizards. Two children dressed as ghosts came skipping across the drawbridge.

'That ought to keep Wailing William, the Castle Ghost, happy,' said Corbie. 'He's always wailing about being on his own. Now he'll have other ghosts to play with tonight, even if they are only pretend ones.'

Bad George and Rude Arabella, Professor Pernickety's two most badly behaved pupils had turned up.

Bad George was with his mum and his baby brother and he was in a very grumpy mood.

Rude Arabella had come along with her gran. Arabella was not only being rude to anyone who spoke to her, she was also being extremely rude to people who *didn't* speak to her.

When the last guest had arrived in the courtyard Jamie gave a mighty blow on his bagpipes. Everyone lined up behind him and he led them towards the Great Hall. As Midden and her team turned to follow their guests, the little witch spoke to Corbie. 'That was good work delivering the party invitations. We can go inside and start the party now. I think all our guests have arrived.'

But Midden was wrong. Not everyone was there.
Someone had been missed out.

When Corbie the Crow was delivering the party
invitations one of the cards had gone astray. This
invitation was for the mischievous Litttle Imp who
lived under the Castle Hill. It had fallen
from Corbie's letter sack right on
top of a bonfire of burning
autumn leaves! The bonfire had
burned up the invitation so quickly
that Corbie hadn't noticed it happening.

So the mischievous Little Imp did not know that he
had been invited to the Hallowe'en Party at Starling
Castle. And he was furious when he heard that everyone else was going.

When he saw all the people arriving at Starling
Castle he was even madder.

Now, from behind one of the pillars in the courtyard,
he watched as the party guests marched into the Great
Hall. When he heard music and the sound of games
beginning, he was raging.

The Little Imp stamped his foot. He glared at the lanterns hanging in the windows. He scowled at the torches and flags on the battlements.

Suddenly he noticed something.

The window at the top of the Tallest Tower was lying open.

The Little Imp knew that was where the Magic Factory workshops were. He also knew that Growl the Gargoyle wasn't on guard duty tonight. Growl was at the Hallowe'en Party and not sitting in his usual place on the window ledge.

Imps are very nimble creatures and it only took this Little Imp a minute to run up the outside of the Tallest Tower. It took him barely one other minute to climb over the windowsill and into the Magic Factory.

There were lots of things to look at and touch in the Magic Factory. Cauldrons and crystal balls waiting to be mended, potions being prepared, spell scrolls and magic books lying open. And then the Little Imp

caught sight of the big cupboard by the fire. He saw the golden key was still in the lock!

Midden had been in such a hurry to go to the Hallowe'en Party that she had forgotten to lock up and put the key away.

In a flash the Little Imp opened the cupboard. He rooted about inside and found the Seven League Boots. He tried them on, but they were too large for him. Next he took down the jar of Magic Dust. But despite trying with all his strength he couldn't get the stopper off. As he reached up to replace the jar he touched something hanging on a hook inside the cupboard. The Little Imp couldn't see anything, but the thing he had touched felt like the shape of a coat or a cloak. He put his hand underneath it to lift it down.

'Oh!' gasped the Little Imp.

His hand had disappeared!

The Little Imp pulled his hand back and he could see it. But when he put his hand under the cloak again he couldn't!

'Aha!' cried the Imp. 'I know what this is.

It's an Invisibility Cloak. If I put it over my head no one will be able to see me. I can go to the Hallowe'en Party and get my own back on them for not inviting me.'

The Bogle was having great fun at the Hallowe'en Party using his Magic Dust to liven things up.

He went to where people were ducking for apples and flung a sprinkle of Magic Dust over the basins. Immediately the apples began to bob up and down in the water splashing each other and crying out:

> *'Duck for apples*
> *Have some fun!*
> *There's enough*
> *For everyone!'*

Then the Bogle saw a group of children being chased by a couple of Vomiting Vampires. He ran after them and blew some Magic Dust at the Vampires. This made the vomit turn into candy floss.

Everyone was having such a good time that nobody noticed the door of the Great Hall open.

Nobody heard the patter of little feet.

Nobody saw the Little Imp.

But he saw *them*.

'Let's see . . . ' The Little Imp looked round.

He saw that it would only take a Little Imp a little effort to play some tricks. What should he do first?

There were various games going on: Ducking for Apples, Pin the Hat on the Wizard, Musical Monsters, or Pass the Pongy Parcel.

At the far end of the hall Bad George was also looking around wondering which game to take part in. He decided on the treacly scone game. The scones had been smothered in black sticky treacle and tied with a length of string to hang down from one of the roof beams. The idea was to eat a scone without using your hands.

Bad George charged over and elbowed some children out of the way. He put his hands behind his back and leaned forward to bite the treacly scone. But, as he opened his mouth, the scone swung over his head.

An invisible hand had pulled the string! The scone turned back, opened up, and nipped George on his bottom!

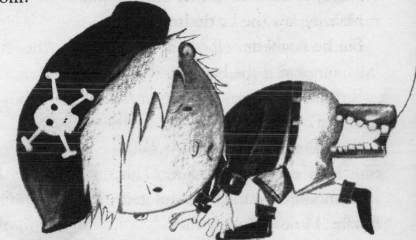

'Oww!!!!' George yelped.

'Hee, hee, hee,' tittered the Little Imp.

'Ow! Ow! Ow!' screeched George. He ran off howling.

'Oh dear,' said Midden when she heard the noise. She went to see what was wrong.

But Bad George's mum had seen him push the other children out of the way and she wasn't giving him any sympathy. 'He says a treacle scone bit him,' she told Midden. 'What nonsense!'

Midden thought it was a very strange story but she

didn't have time to think about it, because it was time to award the prize for the best pumpkin lantern. Holding up their hollowed-out pumpkins the children made their way on to the stage.

Rude Arabella elbowed her way to the front. 'My pumpkin is the biggest,' she declared.

'I think my pumpkin is bigger than yours,' a boy said nervously.

'No, it's not,' said Rude Arabella. She held up her pumpkin. 'The prize should be mine,' she shouted loudly. 'Mine! Mine! Mine!'

'I don't think so, dear,' said Jamie the Drawbridge Keeper, who was the judge. He looked at Arabella's pumpkin. Then he looked again. 'Oh,' he said. 'It does seem bigger than it was a moment ago—' Jamie stopped speaking and stared.

Rude Arabella's pumpkin was growing larger and larger.

Everyone gasped. Nobody heard the Little Imp snigger and whisper in Rude Arabella's ear. 'You wanted a huge pumpkin? Now you will have one!'

The very next second the pumpkin exploded.

Bright orange pumpkin pieces rained down on Rude Arabella. There were pieces on her face, in her hair, in her ears, and one very large piece stuck in her mouth.

'Wu . . . wu . . . wubu,' said Arabella. She ran off the stage and made a signal to her gran to take the piece of pumpkin out of her mouth.

Rude Arabella's gran started to remove the pumpkin from Arabella's mouth. Then she stopped. 'You can't speak with that in your mouth, can you, Arabella?'

Rude Arabella shook her head.

'Well,' said Arabella's gran, 'I think I'll wait a bit before I take it out so that I can have some peace.

Midden had seen what had happened to Bad George and Rude Arabella. She hurried over to where the Bogle was standing.

'You must stop it at once,' she said.

'Stop what?' the Bogle asked her.

'Stop whatever it is you are doing,' said Midden.

'But I'm not doing anything,' said the Bogle.

'You mean to tell me that you haven't used your Magic Dust?' Midden asked him.

'Well yes,' said the Bogle. 'I used it to make the apples talk and I changed the Vomiting Vampire vomit into candy floss.'

'That's all?' asked Midden.

'That's all,' said the Bogle.

'What about these things that are happening?' Midden asked him. 'A treacle scone bit Bad George and now he can't sit down. And Rude Arabella's pumpkin exploded leaving a piece stuck in her mouth so now she can't talk.'

'I thought it was really funny when those things happened,' the Bogle said truthfully. 'But it wasn't me.'

Midden looked at him sharply. The Bogle was very good at mixing things up but he definitely wasn't good at telling fibs.

The Bogle opened his hands—all four of them—and Midden could see that they were empty. His bag of Magic Dust was tucked down the inside of his purple Bogle boot.

Midden looked around the Great Hall. If it wasn't the Bogle making spells, who or what was causing trouble?

The Little Imp chuckled quietly to himself. While he was wearing the Invisibility Cloak Midden would never guess who was playing tricks to spoil the Hallowe'en Party.

The Little Imp raced across the floor of the Great Hall. He'd seen a game of Musical Monsters about to begin and intended to barge in amongst the children.

He laughed as he ran through some gloopy blobs of candy floss lying on the floor. He didn't see that some of it had stuck to his feet.

Midden, who was gazing around trying to find the cause of the trouble, spotted little Impish footprints pattering across the floor.

'Ah!' she said. 'The mischief maker! And I think I know why they are invisible. Let's see who it is!'

Midden took her magic wand from behind her ear.

She raised it in the air. And as she did so, Midden said some magic words.

'*You have once been*
Not seen.
Now be
Where we can see!'

She waved her magic wand.

Zippity Zap!!!

The Invisibility Cloak dropped onto the floor and everyone could see the Little Imp. He was getting ready to jump in among the Musical Monsters.

'You are a naughty Imp,' said Midden in a stern voice.

The Little Imp burst into tears.

At once Midden felt sorry for him. 'Why are you trying to spoil the Hallowe'en Party?' she asked.

'Because you didn't invite me,' sobbed the Little Imp.

'But I *did* invite you,' said Midden. 'I remember writing out your invitation.' She rummaged in the pockets of her witch's cape until she found the party guest list.

'Look. There's your name right there. See?' She pointed to his name. '"Little Imp", right after "Little Bo Peep" and just before "Loch Ness Monster".'

'Thank goodness Nessie couldn't come,' muttered the Bogle. 'There'd be no food left if she'd turned up.'

'Well, I didn't get my invitation,' said the Little Imp.

Corbie the Clever Crow flew over. 'It's my fault,' he cawed. 'I must have dropped it. I'm sorry.'

The Little Imp sniffed. 'I'm sorry, too, for making mischief,' he said.

Midden put her arm around his shoulders. 'I'm going to cut the Hallowe'en cake,' she said. 'Would you like a piece?'

The Little Imp nodded his head.

'You mustn't do naughty things like that again,' said

Midden. 'Look at the people you have upset.'

The Little Imp looked round the Great Hall.

'Where?' he asked.

Midden looked around too.

Rude Arabella's gran seemed quite happy that there was a large piece of pumpkin stuck in Arabella's mouth. And Bad George had been standing quietly in a corner for ten minutes. His mum was telling her friends that it was the longest George had ever gone without bothering anyone.

'Hmmmm,' said Midden. 'Well, maybe you can make amends by helping me give out the cake.'

So the Little Imp made sure that everyone got a slice of Hallowe'en cake. Bad George ate his standing up. Rude Arabella's gran relented and took the piece of pumpkin out of Arabella's mouth so that she could eat hers. When it was time to go home, everyone agreed that it had been the best Hallowe'en Party ever.

'Magical Fantastical,' said the Bogle. 'Magical Fantastical.'

Theresa Breslin is a Carnegie Medal-winning author whose work has appeared on radio and television. She writes books for all age groups and they have been translated into a number of languages. She lives in the middle of Scotland, a short broomstick ride away from Stirling Castle. It was while visiting Stirling Castle that Theresa noticed something strange . . . Stirling Castle is very, very like Starling Castle where the Magic Factory workshops are. So keep a sharp lookout if you ever go there . . .

There's lots more 'Magic Factory' fun
to be had. Why don't you try . . .

COLD SPELL

Four fun stories in which Midden and her friends must
warm up the prince of winter; untangle a magical
mix-up; calm a cross dragon; and undo a dancing spell
—and all before midnight!

Let the Magic Factory cast its spell on you!

There's even more 'Magic Factory' fun
to be had in . . .

MIDSUMMER MAGIC

In these four fun stories, Midden and her friends must catch some scary monsters; cook up a storm in the castle café; help a ghost find his lost voice; and fight a fearsome fire — all before the spectacular summer barbecue!

Let the Magic Factory cast its spell on you!